For my children,

Reginald, Dominique, Tiffany, Noble, Andreu,
Quesette, Jordan, Jonathan, Mia Faye and the village,

you must know where you came from
in order to know where you are going.

Loving you always,

Ya Ya

DOMINIQUE AND THE MIRROR
Book 5: **The Spirit**

ISBN-13: 978-0-692-15163-1 (Cassie's Stories)
ISBN-10: 069215163X

Printed in the United States of America

DOMINIQUE
and the
MIRROR

Book 5

The Spirit

By

Cassie

Illustrations by
Amakubukuro Brown

IT'S MORNING. In the mirror I saw Adedayo and the other freed slaves walk off the ship which had reached Canada. The ship was given to the slaves in Jamaica West Indies by the governor, so that their revolt would not spread to slaves on other plantations throughout the island. Adedayo touched the ground with his feet and said, "I am free". He raised his arms, dropped to his knees and shouted, "Thank you God"! Suddenly, Adedayo went into the seeing. He and I saw the ancestors say, "You have reach the third and final land". You have proven you have the strength of a lion and the wisdom of a king." Adedayo saw his wife and children looking for him. He saw they were also free. The mirror shut down. I went back in my room, sat on my bed and thought about how my mom was acting when the mirror flashed a bright yellow light. Suddenly, I was able to hear everything that was happening in the mirror when Adedayo went into the seeing.

MY MOM called me to the kitchen and said, "Today you will be confronted by a substitute teacher that has a hatred for people of color who are intelligent. This person is filled with darkness and will try to belittle you to make you feel small and worthless which you know you are not. Dominique, you are filled with the light just as I am. When you respond, to this person that is in the dark, what will you say?" When you respond, remember who you are. You can not change the mind of an ignorant person and it is a waste of time to argue". "Mom, I will tell her, I pray that God has mercy on you when he teaches you your lesson."

WHEN I ARRIVED to school we had a substitute teacher! How did my mom know? The teacher made many statements that slavery was a good thing for black people, that it gave them food and a place to live and that they were being taken care of. I was shocked and became angry. I knew what she was saying was not true because of what I have learned through the mirror and my research at the Schaumburg library on the slavery of African people in America. Everything she was saying was insulting and not true. I remembered my mom telling me this morning, "You cannot change the mind of an ignorant person."

I RAISED MY HAND and asked to be excused from class. I went to my principal's office, Mrs. Fitch. In the office I told her secretary that it was urgent I speak to her. She put my request by phone and the response was, "Show Dominique in." I sat down and explained to Mrs. Finch that for a while now I have been interested in researching about my culture. Through my research I have not found at anytime that slavery was a good thing for my ancestors.

Mrs. Finch asked me why am I so upset and what does it have to with slavery. I explained that the person teaching my class had made the statement which infuriated me. I then went on to explain the inhuman ways our ancestors had suffered at the hand of slavery in the United States and Africa. All Mrs. Finch could do was sit at her desk with her mouth open. She was shocked that I knew so much about the subject. I understand that most adults underestimate what children know. Of course she didn't know I have seen all of these things through my mirror. Mrs. Finch said, "I am very impressed that you did not react negatively and you excused yourself from the class and sought help in this situation. I would like for you to return to class and I will be there shortly." I thanked Mrs. Finch and returned to class.

THE SUBSTITUTE TEACHER continued to say offensive things to the class and they started to express their anger. Mrs. Finch walked in the room after the last statement was made. She asked the teacher to step into the hall. The class could not hear what was being said but we could imagine by the expressions on their faces. We saw that the substitute teacher walked in the direction of the office and Mrs. Finch came back into my class. Mrs. Finch apologized for the statements made by the teacher. She then said, "I will put together a curriculum that teaches black history so that those who do not know will learn and understand why your teacher was making the statements she did. The class will also teach you how to protect yourselves with knowledge when you are confronted with ignorance again."

"**NOW, CLASS,** recite what we have taught you to believe about yourself. Who are you?"

"I am great. I am amazing. I am significant. I am smart. I am beautiful. I am special. I stand up with all the confidence in the world. I can look at any man or woman in the face and say I am (say your name) Dominique, No one can stop me but me. The only person that can stand in my way is me and that is not an option. I am great. No one in the world can stop my greatness or shake my confidence. It does not matter what you say about me, it's about how I feel about myself. I love me because I am great." I noticed that we were reciting our school's motto, Mrs. Finch bought in another teacher that started teaching us about black history and there were many things I had not known. This made the class very interesting.

IT WAS LUNCH TIME. As I took the first bite of my sandwich, I thought about my mom. How did she know what was going to happen today?

"Oh, my mother has the seeing!" All of a sudden I started seeing though my eyes! My mother! "I'm seeing without the mirror!" My mother is a little girl, about seven years old. I'm seeing her mother telling her to go to the store and buy a light bulb. She was so happy her mother let her go to the store by herself. She was skipping on her way back from the store and she dropped the bag with the light bulb. It hit the ground and when she looked in the bag, it was in many pieces. I was seeing how she became very frightened. Suddenly, for the first time, she started praying to God. She was thanking God for not getting in trouble for dropping the bag. When she walked in the apartment and told her mother, her mother just gave her more money and sent her back to the store. Her mother said, "Be very careful this time." I saw how my mother was very happy and realized God answered her prayer. From that day on she spoke to God often and not just when she thought she would get in trouble.

AFTER SCHOOL I ran home. Both my mom and dad were home. I called a family meeting and everybody came into the living room. They were both smiling! They knew! I explained what happened today, including what mom told me this morning. Dad said, "I know you are excited. Yes we know: you can see. You are around the age when your mom and I were able to see. It is our family's gift. You have it now, just as Adedayo had the seeing. You know about Adedayo?" Dad said, "You don't need the mirror any more. Take care of it." I said I will. "And, last thing: do not tell anyone about your gift. If you do, you will not like the outcome." My mom and dad hugged me and I then went into my room.

I LIED in my bed thinking about everything that happened today and about the mirror. I blinked and started seeing Adedayo in Canada. Freed slaves walked up to him and the others who had gotten off the ship, helping them with there needs, food, clothing and lodging. You see as in Africa, the natives in their village lived by the word, "Ubuntu" (oǒ'boǒntoō) how can one of us be happy if all others are sad. The freed slaves, no matter what they have been through, continued the way of living as a village.

A FREE SLAVE named George took Adedayo to meet and stay with his family and to teach him the way of living free. George took him to his home where Adedayo met his wife Janie and their baby Gussie. Adedayo ate and rested. George took him to the waterfront the next day to get work that he would be paid for. They both met with Mr. Templeton who was a fisherman. He owned his own boat and sold the fish he caught. George said to Mr. Templeton, My friend is looking for work," and Mr. Templeton hired Adedayo on the spot. That night at George's house Adedayo saw in the seeing that his wife and children were in a place called Preston in Nova Scotia. He had asked George where the town Preston was. He told him it was one of the delivery stops Mr. Templeton made every other day. Adedayo was overjoyed that he would soon see his family. The next day Adedayo explained everything that happened to him and his family to Mr. Templeton. He felt so bad for him. The next morning he took Adedayo with him to Preston in Nova Scotia.

WHEN THEY ARRIVED, Mr. Templeton went to a family that owned a grocery store and asked them if they knew of a Sally Sawyer, Adedayo's family. The owner of the store told them to wait in the store. He sent his delivery man out. When the delivery man came back, Sadie, his wife, who was now called Sally Sawyer, and the children were with him. Adedayo ran to his family, hugged and kissed them.

AFTER ADEDAYO found his family he stepped outside for a moment and said, "The God of Abraham accepted my offer of the mirror and answered my prayer. He saved my family!"

and a New Beginning

www.ingramcontent.com/pod-product-compliance
Lightning Source LLC
Chambersburg PA
CBHW041008170626
46815CB00002B/206